PETER H. REYNOLDS

# The North Star

CANDLEWICK PRESS

To all the parents and educators of the world,
and to those who are brave enough to
follow their dreams

First Candlewick Press edition 2009
First published in 1997 by FableVision

Library of Congress Cataloging-in-Publication Data is available.

Library of Congress Catalog Card Number 2008935652

ISBN 978-0-7636-3677-7

10 11 12 13 14 15 SCP 10 9 8 7 6 5

Printed in Humen, Dongguan, China

This book was typeset in Gararond.
The illustrations were done in ink and watercolor.

Candlewick Press
99 Dover Street
Somerville, Massachusetts 02144

visit us at www.candlewick.com

Dear Friend,

What wondrous things books can be. My favorites are ones that move me—to laughter, to tears, to deep thought, and to action.

*The North Star* is a story for all ages. Whether you are beginning a new journey, have decided to alter the direction of your life, or are starting out for the first time, this book is here to encourage you. Take a moment to slow down to a more thoughtful pace, to ponder, reflect, imagine, and envision. Take the time to believe in your dreams, to celebrate possibility.

It is my hope that whatever *The North Star* may spark in you will continue to shine—both for you and those around you—as you navigate your very own wonderful journey.

Keep the book close at hand, and when you need that gentle reminder to keep your dreams in view, open and revisit it.

This is my gift to you. Listen carefully and you will hear not my voice, but yours.

Wishing you a stellar journey,

*Peter H. Reynolds*

A sweet breeze
met the boy
as he awoke to his journey.

He traveled on all fours for quite some time . . .
and he grew.

And he paused.

One day he had the urge to stand . . . to walk.

It made his journey easier.
He could run, too.
But for the most part, he walked.
He wasn't afraid of much.

He wandered the fields, exploring,
sometimes stopping . . .

sometimes going happily in
circles, sometimes dancing. . . .

Sometimes napping.

One day the boy saw an oak leaf drift
and land on the water.

He wondered how the leaf
managed to float . . . the way the stars
seemed to float in the night sky.

A spray of sand interrupted his thoughts.

"Where are you going in such a hurry?" asked the boy.

But the rabbit shot out of sight, disappearing onto
a path the boy had never noticed before.

The boy left the floating leaf and wandered
toward the path. There he saw a cat.

The cat purrrred gently.

"Where did the rabbit go in such a hurry?"
the boy asked the cat.

"He was in a rush to start his journey.
It's time for you to start your journey, too."

"Oh, but I *have* been on a journey!" the boy cried.
"I've seen many wonderful things.
Some I understand, and some I don't . . .
like how that leaf floats on the water."

"Well, that's fascinating,
but I'd hate for you to be late.
You don't want to be left behind."

"Behind? Who's ahead of me?"

"You wouldn't believe how many!
You know, you're not the only one on this journey.
Plenty ahead of you. Lots to follow."

The boy began walking down the path.
It stretched out far ahead of him.

Signs kept pointing him along the way.
Some parts of the journey were easy,
and some were very difficult.

Although he was following the well-worn path,
he had a growing feeling that he was lost.

The forest seemed to be growing thicker.
The soil was wet and muddy, making every step a struggle.
Clouds had rolled in overhead,
and the darkness closed in around him.

After many difficult miles,
he could not take another step.
He noticed an oak leaf drift from the sky.
It sailed with ease.

It swirled on a breeze and was carried deep into the forest.
The leaf disappeared behind a grove of trees.

He stepped off the path to follow it.

The boy found the leaf floating on a pond in a peaceful clearing, like a delicate boat on a dreamy voyage.

His thoughts were interrupted by a voice—

"Oh! There you are! I was worried," said the cat.
"Don't wander off like that!

Now, hurry. You're falling behind!"

So the boy ran . . . and ran . . . and ran. . . . And as he ran,
he noticed the forest getting darker and thicker.

The muddy ground became covered with water.
He could no longer see the path.

He sloshed through the swamp . . .

until he came to a clearing in the forest. There he saw . . .

a bird.

"You look lost," the bird said.

"I don't think so. I mean, I'm not sure if I'm lost,"
the boy replied. "I really hadn't thought about it."

"Hadn't thought about it?" said the bird.
"You must have some idea of where you're going, yes?"

"Well . . . I've been following the path.

It seems as if many people have taken it before me,
and there have been many signs along the way . . .

and a very helpful cat guided me back to the path
when I started to wander."

The crickets fell silent as the bird asked,
"But where do *you* want to be going?"

"I'm not sure," said the boy as he looked around
at the dark, tangled swamp, "but I do know that *this*
isn't where I want to be. I guess I *am* lost."

The bird said, "Ask yourself where it is you want to go,
and then follow the signs you already know."

"What signs? Where are they?"

But the bird flew off into the cloudy night sky.
The boy looked up into the sky—
something he had not done in a very, very long time.
He tried desperately to see where the bird had gone.
And as he did, the clouds seemed to melt . . .
and there above him . . .

was a star, a very bright star.

The boy stared at the star and felt a pang in his heart,
a tingling in his spine, a whisper in his ear.
*He could hear the star.*
The voice sounded so familiar.

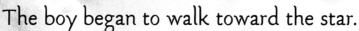

The boy began to walk toward the star.
As he did, he noticed many other stars
stretched out above him like a great big map.
They had been there all along, waiting for him.
He stopped and rested a moment,
savoring his guiding stars.

"What are you staring at?" croaked a voice behind him.
"What is up there? What's so interesting?"

The boy waded closer and answered,
"Stars. I'm looking at the stars."

"What stars?" asked the frog.
"I see a dark sky and mist and low, green clouds."

"You don't see them?" the boy asked.
"They're helping guide me out of the swamp.
Would you like to come with me?"

"No, thank you." The frog smiled.
"I'm quite at home here in the bog.
I swam here as a tadpole and grew up here,
and here I will stay."

The boy realized at that moment that
everyone has a different journey, different signs—
and different stars. Their own constellations.

The boy left the frog, who croaked a farewell:
"Good luck on your journey."

As he ventured beyond the swampy forest,
the boy heard a cry.

It was the rabbit who had been in such a hurry earlier,
looking tired and hungry. He was stranded on a limb
in the middle of the rushing river.

The boy waded out but realized that the river was too deep.
The rabbit was trapped.

Then he saw an oak leaf drift by.
It gave him an idea.

The boy fashioned a boat out of swamp grass
and twigs and rescued the rabbit.

The boy smiled, having helped make
the rabbit's journey easier.

The boy looked up.
He noticed that the star had become even brighter.

He followed the star, and as he did, the muddy ground
grew drier . . . then grassy . . . then soft and sandy.

Finally he came to rest atop a dune.

There below him was a beach . . . and a boat.

The boy looked out toward the horizon.

The star glowed steadily, reminding him that
he still had a long journey ahead.
But it was his own journey,
his very own wonderful journey.

# The Beginning